Goodnight,

Every evening, when the sun slowly sets and other folk are going to bed, Jacob the Sandman wakes up and starts work.

But one evening, when the sun slowly set, Jacob gave an enormous yawn, rolled over and slipped back into his warm, fuzzy dream. He dreamed he was riding a sheep over a hill made of delicious pistachio ice cream.

"Wake up, Jacob! Wake up!" Milo the mouse shook Jacob until he fell off his sheep, out of his dream, out of bed and onto the floor.

"What?! Milo! What on earth's the matter?"

"Jacob! You've overslept!" squeaked Milo. "Look out the window: the sun has set, the owls are already awake and we should be collecting magic dream sand!"

As fast as he could, Jacob pulled on his coat and hat. At the door he sleepily remembered his lantern. The Sandman always carries a lantern to find his way through the dark night.

Jacob and Milo hurried through the forest
to Dream Sand Hill.

Every night when the moon rises, it sprinkles
magic dream sand on Dream Sand Hill, and every
night Jacob the Sandman gathers the sand. He
scatters it over the houses of sleeping children,
so they will dream their happiest dreams.

But on *this* night, Jacob and Milo were late,
and as they drew near Dream Sand Hill,
they heard a strange sound…

It was the most thunderous snoring they'd ever known!
And in the moonlight they could see an odd, spiky shape on
the hilltop.

Then Milo realised who was snoring on Dream Sand Hill.
It was the Night Monster! And he was lying right in the
sprinkling of magic dream sand.

"Oh dear, oh dear! What a disaster!" squeaked Milo.

Do you know the Night Monster? Sometimes he hides in children's bedrooms and gives them a fright if they wake in the dark.

Jacob and Milo looked at his fangs and quaked.

Then Jacob whispered bravely, "Well, he *is* asleep. Maybe we can gather some dream sand very quietly, and sneak away?"

But, *oh no…*

Roused by the light from Jacob's lantern, the Night Monster opened one big pale eye.

"Why did you wake me up?" he grumbled. "I was
having the most wonderful happy dream." He stumbled
sleepily to his feet.

Jacob and Milo both wanted to run down the hill away
from the grumbling, stumbling Night Monster. They
knew, though, that all the children asleep that night
needed magic dream sand to dream happy dreams.

Jacob thought hard.

"Night Monster," he said, "you cannot sleep on
Dream Sand Hill because we have to gather the sand.
But listen: I will let you keep a handful of dream sand,
if you promise you will never frighten children again!"

Milo thought Jacob was very very brave indeed.

"You don't understand." The Night Monster sighed sadly. "I don't want to frighten children. I just visit them because I hate being alone at night. I'm so afraid of the dark." He sniffed. "And besides, children always have the comfiest, cosiest bedrooms."

Then the Night Monster began to cry.

Jacob and Milo were very surprised, and they started to feel sorry for him.

"Maybe… maybe I could come along with you?"
the Night Monster asked. "Oh please, Sandman,
let me help you scatter the magic dream sand!"

Jacob thought hard. He was very late tonight;
he could certainly do with some extra help.

"Yes," he said finally. "You can come along with
Milo and me."

Working together, Jacob, Milo and the
Night Monster gathered the sand faster than
ever before, and were soon on their way.

They drifted through the starry sky in Jacob's purple hot-air balloon. When the moon shone brightest, the Sandman and his two helpers scattered magic dream sand over all the sleeping children, bringing them wonderful happy dreams.

"Do you know, Night Monster," said Jacob, as they were floating homewards, "I've decided you should live at our house. Milo and I could build you a comfy, cosy bedroom of your very own."

"And do you know, Night Monster," added Milo, "I've decided you need a new name. What about Albie?"

"It's a beautiful name!" replied Albie, delighted. "Can we start on my new room tomorrow?"

"Yes, tomorrow!" agreed Jacob.

As the morning sun rose, Jacob kicked off his boots, Milo flopped down on his favourite cushion, and Albie closed his heavy eyes, smiling a big, happy smile. Soon they were fast asleep, dreaming of riding sheep over delicious, green pistachio-ice-cream hills.

The Sandman's Song

I'll bring you horses made of gold,
Magic castles grand and old,
Princes, knights, fairy-queens, dragons, nightingales –
Great adventures and favourite tales.
Princes, knights, fairy-queens, dragons, nightingales –
Great adventures and favourite tales.

For every night, I float to you,
And the other children too.
Over roofs, scatter dreams, scatter magic sand,
Through the sleeping and peaceful land.
Over roofs, scatter dreams, scatter magic sand,
Through the sleeping and peaceful land.